FISH

Joanne Randolph

PowerKiDS press™

New York

Published in 2007 by The Rosen Publishing Group, Inc.
29 East 21st Street, New York, NY 10010

First Edition

Book Design: Julio Gil

Photo Credits: Cover, pp. 1, 5, 7, 9, 11, 13, 17, 19, 21 Shutterstock.com; p. 15 © www.istockphoto.com/Donna Lorka.

Library of Congress Cataloging-in-Publication Data

Randolph, Joanne.
  Fish / Joanne Randolph. — 1st ed.
     p. cm. — (Classroom pets)
  Includes bibliographical references and index.
  ISBN-13: 978-1-4042-3681-3 (library binding)
  ISBN-10: 1-4042-3681-3 (library binding)
  1. Aquarium fishes—Juvenile literature. I. Title.

SF457.25.R36 2007
597'.073—dc22

                                    2006031056

Manufactured in the United States of America

Contents

Picking a Fish for Your Classroom

Imagine watching colorful fish swim among the plants and rocks in their watery home. If you bring fun, beautiful fish into your classroom, you will see this every day.

It is important to do some **research** before you take your pet home, though. What kinds of fish do you and your classmates want? Will the different fish you pick get along? Do they have the same needs, such as the kind of food they eat or how warm the water needs to be? Find out the answers to these questions, and you will soon be the owners of happy classroom pets.

This is a lionhead goldfish. Lionhead goldfish will eat most kinds of food and they like cold freshwater.

About Fish

Fish have been swimming in Earth's waters for hundreds of millions of years. Some fish live in the salty water of the oceans. Other fish live in freshwater. There are around 25,000 different **species** of fish today. You will not find most of these living as pets, though.

Tropical fish are top picks, because they are colorful and fun to watch. Other kinds of fish make good pets, too, though. For example, many people keep goldfish, which like cool freshwater. No matter what kind of fish you pick, you need to find out what these fish need to live long, healthy lives.

The regal tang likes warm, salty water. This fish moves around a lot and needs a tank with lots of space.

So Many Fish

Some of the best-liked fish are those that live in tropical freshwater. These fish include barbs, danios, tetras, oscars, and bettas. The next most common fish kept as pets are tropical saltwater fish. Some of the fish that like warm, salty water are clownfish, butterflyfish, damselfish, surgeons, and tangs.

Many people also like to keep coldwater fish. Some well-liked fish that live in cold freshwater are goldfish, koi, sunfish, sticklebacks, and minnows. Some fish that like cold salt water are blennies, gobies, wrasses, and scorpionfish. There are so many fish that make great pets.

The betta called the Siamese fighting fish is commonly kept as a pet. This fish will fight and try to kill other fish of the same kind.

Do Not Crowd Me!

The best home for your fish depends on what kind of fish you pick for your classroom. All pet fish need an **aquarium**, though. There are many different sizes and shapes. Your class will likely want to pick a mid-sized or large aquarium shaped like a rectangle. You will also need special tools, such as filters, lights, a heater, and a **thermometer**.

Your fish will need space, so do not get too many for one tank. Having fewer fish in your tank cuts down on fighting. It also keeps the water cleaner.

Larger tanks are easier to care for. This large tank is filled with colorful stones and plants and a good number of fish.

A Fitting Home

Besides the tools you need to move the water, heat it, and keep it clean, there are many other things you can put in your tank. Some fish do not mind a tank without much in it. Others feel safer if there are plants, rocks, and hiding places. Some fish like to dig into the bottom of their home. These fish will be happy if you cover the tank bottom with small rocks.

Try to make a home that is like the fish's natural **habitat**. A fitting home will make for some happy fish classmates.

The lionfish will be happy in a home that is like the warm, salty waters of the coral reef, where it lives in the wild.

What is one of the most important rules of fish ownership? Do not overfeed your fish. You should feed your fish only what they will eat in a few minutes. Anything extra will just rot and cause problems in your tank. The kind of food your fish eats depends on what kind of fish you have picked.

Most pet stores sell foods that have everything your fish needs to stay healthy. Some of the common foods are **pellets**, flakes, and dried shrimp. You should try to feed your fish food that is like what it would eat in the wild.

This koi is about to eat a food pellet. Koi are commonly kept in outdoor ponds, but they can be kept in indoor aquariums, too.

Caring for Your Fish

Part of how you care for your fish has to do with what kind of fish you pick. A fish that lives in tropical freshwater needs different care from one that lives in cold salt water. All fish need clean homes, the right kind of water, and food, though.

Someone in the class needs to check the **temperature** of the water each day. Some fish will die if the temperature changes too much. Keep an eye on the filter, too. Clean it or change it when it becomes dirty. These are just a few ways you can care for your new pet.

You and your classmates must keep the tank clean. Taking out old water and adding new water is one way to keep your fish healthy.

Fish in Action

Fish are not warm and fuzzy. They still make interesting pets, though. Watch your fish in action. You may see them become more **active** when you get close to the tank. They have learned that you feed them, and they are letting you know they like that!

You will also see that some fish swim in groups, called schools. Other fish like to hide among the rocks or plants. Still others like to lie along the bottom. Can you find out why some fish act the way they do? You have a lot to learn from your new friends.

Catfish like to spend their time along the bottom looking for food.
This catfish needs to eat lots of green foods each day.

A Healthy Pet

Your new classroom pet needs you to keep it healthy and happy. Everyone in the class needs to take **responsibility** for the care and safety of the fish. Spend time with the fish each day. If you think any of the fish are sick, let your teacher know. Some things to look out for are problems with the skin or fins. Many illnesses in fish can be fixed by making changes to the water.

A healthy fish has strong colors and healthy-looking skin. The eyes should be clear. The fins should stand up tall, not droop. If the fish seems to be having trouble swimming, it may be sick, too.

This is a healthy goldfish. Its fins are standing up, and its skin looks bright and shiny.

In the Classroom

Fish can be beautiful, interesting pets. Your class can learn a lot about these animals that live in Earth's waters.

Make a natural home for your fish. Then watch what it does. Draw pictures of your fish in its habitat. Make a story to go with the pictures. This story can tell people all about the fishy friend that shares your class. Your story can also talk about how you care for the fish each day. You have a chance to peek into a watery world that many people never get to see up close. This makes you and your classmates very lucky.

Glossary

active (AK-tiv) Busy or moving.

aquarium (uh-KWAYR-ee-um) A place where animals that live in water are kept for study and show.

habitat (HA-beh-tat) The place or kind of land where an animal or a plant naturally lives.

pellets (PEH-lutz) Small, round things.

research (REE-serch) Careful study.

responsibility (rih-spon-sih-BIH-lih-tee) Something that a person must take care of or finish.

species (SPEE-sheez) One kind of living thing. All people are one species.

temperature (TEM-pur-cher) How hot or cold something is.

thermometer (ther-MAH-meh-ter) A tool used to measure how hot or cold something is.

tropical (TRAH-puh-kul) Having to do with the warm parts of Earth.

Index

Web Sites

Due to the changing nature of Internet links, PowerKids Press has developed an online list of Web sites related to this book. This site is updated regularly. Please use this link to access the list:
www.powerkidslinks.com/cpets/fish/